Mel Bay Presents

Solo Pieces

for the
INTERMEDIATE
VIOLINIST

By Craig Duncan

1 2 3 4 5 6 7 8 9 0

CONTENTS

	Violin	Piano

Air from "The Water Music" 18 34
Georg Friederic Handel

Allegro 9 16
Wolfgang A. Mozart

Allegro from Sonata Opus 6, Number 7 . . . . 14 26
Tomaso Albinoni

Bouree from "The Royal Fireworks" 8 14
Georg Friederic Handel

Can Can 16 30
Jacques Offenbach

Espana Waltz 4 6
Emil Waldteufel

Gavotta Opus 2, Number 11 . . . . 11 20
Antonio Vivaldi

Marche from "The Nutcracker" 20 38
Peter Tschaikowsky

Minuet In F 7 12
Wolfgang A. Mozart

Minuet In F 7 13
Georg Friederic Handel

On Wings of Song 3 3
Felix Mendelssohn

Tarantella Napoletana 19 36
Traditional Italian

To A Wild Rose 6 10
Edward McDowell

Traumerei 10 18
Robert Schumann

Trumpet Tune 12 22
Henry Purcell

Winter from "The Four Seasons" 13 24
Antonio Vivaldi

On Wings of Song

Felix Mendelssohn

Espana Waltz

Emil Waldteufel

D.C. al Fine

D.C. al Fine

9

To a Wild Rose

Edward A. MacDowell

11

Minuet in F

Wolfgang A. Mozart

Minuet in F

Georg Friederic Handel

Bourree
from "The Royal Fireworks"

Georg Friederic Handel

Allegro

Wolfgang Amadeus Mozart

16

Traumerei

Robert Schumann

Gavotta
from Opus 2, Number 11

Antonio Vivaldi

Trumpet Tune

Henry Purcell

The Four Seasons - Winter

Antonio Vivaldi

Allegro

from Sonata Op. VI, No. 7

Tomaso Albinoni

Can Can

Jacques Offenbach

Air
from "The Water Music"

George Frideric Handel

Tarantella Napoletana

Italian

Marche
from The Nutcracker Suite

Peter Tschaikowsky